The Trees Stand Shining

Poetry of the North American Indians

The Trees Stand Shining

Selected by Hettie Jones

Paintings by Robert Andrew Parker

Dial Books New York

For Nancy of the Eastern Woodlands

Published by Dial Books

A Division of Penguin Books USA Inc.

375 Hudson Street

New York, New York 10014

Text copyright © 1971 by Hettie Jones

Paintings copyright © 1971 by Robert Andrew Parker

All rights reserved

Printed in the U.S.A.

Reissue, 1993

Typography by Atha Tehon

Library of Congress Catalog Card Number: 79-142452

ISBN 0-8037-9083-X   ISBN 0-8037-9084-8

1 2 3 4 5 6 7 8 9 10

The acknowledgments appear on the last page.

The poems in this book are really songs. There are different kinds: some are prayers, some short stories, some lullabies, a few are war chants. In their singing American Indians told how they felt about the world, all they saw in the land, what they did in their lives.

How Indian people spoke was important, too. "My father went on talking to me in a low voice," a Papago woman said once. "That is how our people always talk to their children, so low and quiet, the child thinks he is dreaming. But he never forgets."

The songs collected here have been sung by many, many generations of people. But it wasn't until the nineteenth century that they were translated from the Indian languages and written down.

My Sun!
My Morning Star!
Help this child to become a man.
I name him
Rain-dew Falling!
I name him
Star Mountain!

Tewa

You, whose day it is,
Make it beautiful.
Get out your rainbow colors,
So it will be beautiful.

Nootka

The sunbeams stream forward, dawn boys,
with shimmering shoes of yellow.

Mescalero Apache

At the rainbow spring
The dragonflies start . . .

Zuñi

The mockingbird, the mockingbird,
In the morning he speaks, in the morning
  he sings.
For the sake of the people in the morning
  he speaks,
In the morning he sings.

Acoma

I wonder if everyone is up.
It is morning.
We are alive, so thanks be.
Rise up! Look about!
Go see the horses!

Nez Percé

The broad woods
Grown up to bushes again.
Beautiful plain,
Protruding stone.
Between two lines
Two families in a long-house,
    one at each end.

Iroquois

The deer, the deer, here he went,
Here are his tracks over mother earth . . .
Tramping, tramping, through the deep forest.

Cochiti

Father,
All these he has made me own,
The trees and the forests
Standing
In their places.

Teton Sioux

When the day is cloudy,
The thunder makes a low rumble
And the rain patters against the lodge,
Then it's fine and nice to sleep,
  isn't it?

Crow

Don't you ever,
You up in the sky,
Don't you ever get tired
Of having the clouds between
  you and us?

Nootka

A wolf
I considered myself,
But the owls are hooting
And the night I fear.

Teton Sioux

Who is this?
Who is this?
Giving light
On the top of my lodge.

It is I—the little owl,
    coming,
It is I—the little owl,
    coming,
Down! Down!

Chippewa

Here am I
Behold me
It said as it rose,
I am the moon
Behold me.

Teton Sioux

Mad coyote
Madly sings,
Then roars the west wind!

Tewa

The old men
Say
The earth
Only
Endures,
You spoke
Truly,
You are right.

Teton Sioux

At the edge of the world
It is growing light.
The trees stand shining.
I like it.
It is growing light.

Papago

The eagle speaks

The sun's rays
Lie along my wings
And stretch beyond their tips.

A little gray whirlwind
Is trying to catch me.
Across my path
It keeps whirling.

Papago

As my eyes
Search the prairie,
I feel the summer in the spring.

Chippewa

A little yellow cricket
At the roots of the corn
Is hopping about and singing.

Papago

The little red spiders
And the little gray horned toad
Together they make the rain to fall,
They make the rain to fall.

Papago

Butterfly, butterfly, butterfly, butterfly,
Oh look, see it hovering among the flowers,
It is like a baby trying to walk
    and not knowing how to go. . . .

Acoma

To the Cedar Tree

Look at me, friend!
I come to ask for your dress . . .

I come to beg you for this,
Long-life Maker,
For I am going to make a basket for
    lily roots out of you.
I pray you, friend, not to feel angry. . . .

Kwakiutl

A young man going to war
Gave me his hand
And in it
I found
A yellow bracelet.

Cheyenne-Arapaho

The Black Snake Wind came to me,
The Black Snake Wind came to me.
Came and wrapped itself about
Came here running with its song.

Pima

Friend,
My horse
Flies like a bird
As it runs.

Teton Sioux

They are sailing on the breeze
My feathers
E he!

Chippewa

An eagle feather I see,
A brave I have caught!

Chippewa

Brave Buffalo
I am
I come

Hu–ka–he!

Teton Sioux

The Sioux women
Pass to and fro wailing
As they gather up
Their wounded men.
The voice of their weeping
Comes back to us.

Chippewa

My children,
When at first I liked the whites,
I gave them fruits,
I gave them fruits.

Father have pity on me,
I am crying for thirst,
All is gone,
I have nothing to eat.

I'yehé! my children . . .
The whites are crazy—Ahe'yuhe'yu!

We shall live again.
We shall live again.

Arapaho-Comanche

A voice
I will send
Hear me
The land
All over
A voice
I am sending
Hear me
I will live.

Teton Sioux

"I wonder if everyone is up": from Franz Boas, ed., *Folk Tales of Salishan and Shaptin Tribes*, American Folklore Society, New York, 1917. Reprinted by permission.

"To the cedar tree": from Franz Boas, tr., *35th Annual Report* of the Bureau of American Ethnology, Smithsonian Institution, Washington, 1921. Reprinted by permission.

"Father, all these he has made me own"; "The old men"; "A wolf I considered myself"; "Here I am"; "Friend my horse"; "Brave buffalo"; "A voice I will send." (Bulletin #61: *Teton Sioux Music*). "As my eyes search the prairie"; "An eagle feather I see"; "They are sailing on the breeze"; "The Sioux women." (Bulletin #53: *Chippewa Music*). "You, whose day it is"; "Don't you ever." (Bulletin #124: *Nootka and Quileute Music*). "At the rainbow spring"; "The deer, the deer"; "Butterfly, butterfly." (Bulletin #165): from Frances Densmore, tr. Bulletins of the Bureau of American Ethnology, Smithsonian Institution, Washington. Reprinted by permission.

"A young man going to war": from Frances Densmore, Paper #10, *Cheyenne and Arapaho Music*. Courtesy of the Southwest Museum.

"The sunbeams stream forward": from Pliny Earle Goddard, tr., *Gotal: A Mescalero Apache Ceremony*, Putnam Anniversary Volume, Stechert, New York, 1909.

"When the day is cloudy": from Robert H. Lowie, tr., *The Religion of the Crow Indians*, Vol. 25, Anthropological Papers of the Museum of Natural History, 1922. Reprinted by permission.

"My children": from James Mooney, *14th Annual Report* of the Bureau of American Ethnology, Smithsonian Institution, Washington, 1896. Reprinted by permission.

"The Black Snake Wind came to me": from Frank Russell, tr., *26th Annual Report* of the Bureau of American Ethnology, Smithsonian Institution, Washington, 1908. Reprinted by permission.

"My Sun! My Morning Star!": from Herbert J. Spinden, *Songs of the Tewa*, Exposition of Indian Tribal Arts, 1933.

"The eagle speaks"; "At the edge of the world"; "The little red spiders"; "A little yellow cricket": from Ruth Underhill, *Singing for Power, The Song Magic of the Papago Indians of Southern Arizona*, Berkeley, University of California Press, 1938. Reprinted by permission.

Quote from Papago woman in introduction: from Ruth Underhill, *Memoirs*, Vol. 46, "Autobiography of a Papago Woman." The American Anthropological Association, 1936.